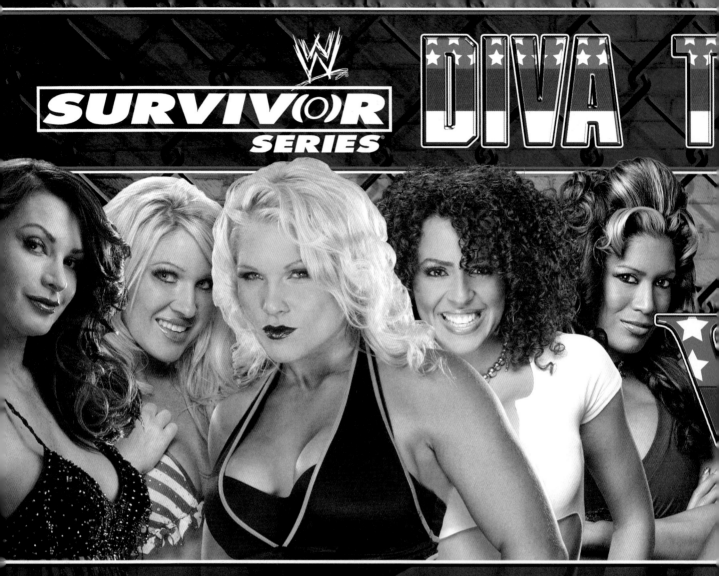

SURVIVOR SERIES

DIVA T

Few Divas in WWE history can compare to the "Glamazon," Beth Phoenix. The Women's Champion says she is the epitome of beauty, class and athleticism and has proven it since she burst on the scene earlier this year. She settles for nothing less than perfection and will expect nothing less when she leads Jillian Hall, Melina, Victoria & Layla into an inter-promotional 10 Diva Tag Team Match against Mickie James, Maria, Torrie Wilson, Michelle McCool & Kelly Kelly at *Survivor Series*.

The "Glamazon" is not known to work well with others – she doesn't need to – but she has one thing in common with her fellow Divas from *Raw*, *SmackDown*, and *ECW*. They all have a chip on their beautiful shoulders.

Nevertheless, there will be some personal issues that may highlight this match. Kelly Kelly wants to lay her claws into her former Extreme Exposé team mate Layla, who, along with The Miz, has made her life a living hell in *ECW*, while Michelle

G TEAM MATCH

McCool and Victoria have been at each other's throats for months on *SmackDown*.

Still, the "Glamazon's" team may have an advantage. She has two other former Women's Champions on her team in Melina and Victoria. One thing is certain, the Divas will add some sugar and spice, and everything nice at *Survivor Series*.

AND THERE'S THE BELL!

"Well here we go, Cole, with the 10 Diva Tag Team Match!"

"Damn it, Cole! Control yourself! Show some respect!"

"I can't wait for this one to get going, partner!"

"Believe me, John. I respect each and every one of the WWE Divas, especially the WWE Women's Champion, Beth Phoenix, who is making her way down to the ring right now!"

"The 'Glamazon,' Beth Phoenix, has been dominating the Women's Division since she captured the title from Candice Michelle several months ago."

"She certainly is quite the imposing woman!"

"She would snap you like a twig, Cole, given half a chance!"

"And here comes Layla straight from ECW!"

"That is one hell of an entrance she is making, Cole! Is it getting hot in here?"

"Speaking of hot entrances, check this out, JBL! Here comes Melina!"

"No one makes an entrance quite like the delicious Melina!"

"Well all the 'Glamazon's' team is in the ring!"

"Just about, Cole!"

"...nd here ...ome their ...position, ...arting off with ...e former ...omen's ...ampion, ...ickie James!"

"The fans here at *Survivor Series* just love this girl, and it is easy to see why!"

"Here's the rest of Mickie's teammates; Torrie Wilson, Kelly Kelly, Michelle McCool and Maria!"

"They all seem pretty pleased to be here! Let's get this thing started!"

"Michelle McCool and Victoria start things off here, and McCool hits Victoria with a great snap suplex!"

"Michelle McCool makes the tag to Torrie Wilson, who comes into the ring and delivers a flying clothesline to Victoria!"

"McCool has been working really hard to improve her in-ring skills, and it shows!"

"What a great move!"

"Victoria retaliates with a huge sidewalk slam which leaves Torrie gasping for breath!"

"You're right, Cole, that move will knock the wind right out of you!"

"Victoria may be looking for the tag here!"

"Torrie Wilson fights her way out, and both women make the tag!"

"Here comes Kelly Kelly and Jillian Hall! Jillian with a huge boot to the gut!"

"Jillian whips Kelly Kelly into the corner."

"Jillian looking for the big splash in the corner...but Kelly Kelly gets her feet up and catches Jillian right in the mouth!"

"That's not going to feel good, Cole!"

"Kelly Kelly going for the roll-up!"

"One...two...Jillian kicks out at two! That was close!"

"Kelly Kelly pulls Jillian over to her corner and makes the tag to Maria!"

"That is some smart tag team tactics there, Cole!"

"Maria sends Jillian into the ropes and catches her with a huge back elbow!"

"What impact, Cole!"

"What is Maria looking for here? Some kind of head scissors manoeuvre perhaps?"

"Whatever it was, it didn't work. Jillian makes the tag and Layla and Melina double team Maria!"

"Maria is in a bad situation here!"

"She needs to get out of that corner is she wants to stay in this match!"

9

"Maria fights her way out of the corner and makes the tag to Mickie James!"

"Mickie looks like a woman on a mission as she takes Melina down with a Lou Thesz Press!"

"Wait a second, Cole! What is this?"

"And she follows up by sending Melina into the corner with some force!"

"Beth Phoenix has Mickie tied up in some sort of tarantula submission hold from the outside!"

"Wow! Melina hit that top turnbuckle like a truck hitting a wall!"

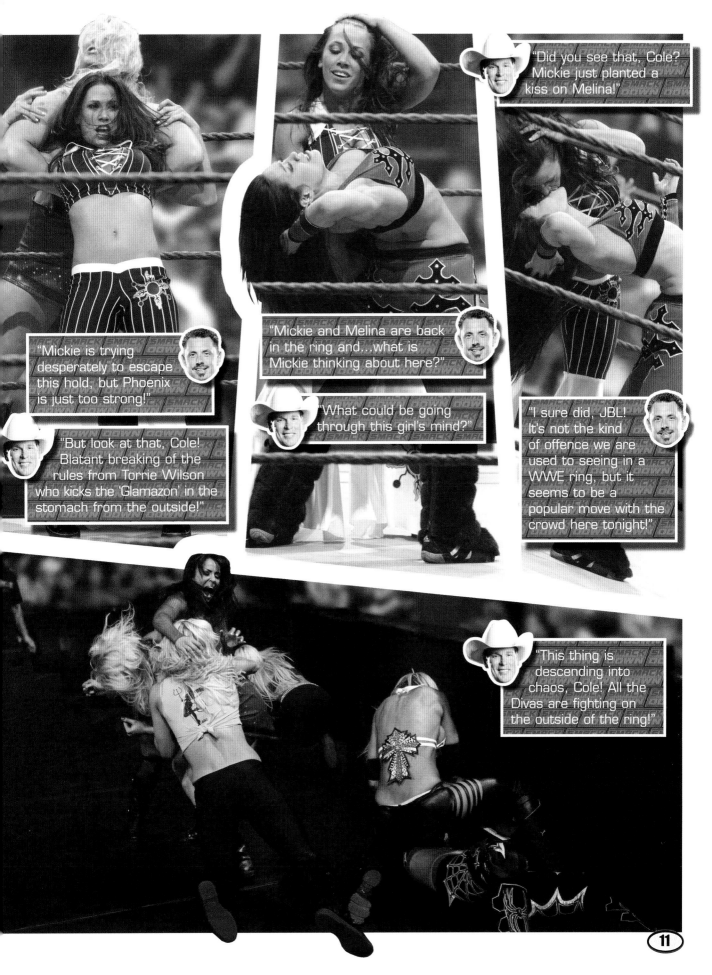

"Did you see that, Cole? Mickie just planted a kiss on Melina!"

"Mickie is trying desperately to escape this hold, but Phoenix is just too strong!"

"But look at that, Cole! Blatant breaking of the rules from Torrie Wilson who kicks the 'Glamazon' in the stomach from the outside!"

"Mickie and Melina are back in the ring and...what is Mickie thinking about here?"

"What could be going through this girl's mind?"

"I sure did, JBL! It's not the kind of offence we are used to seeing in a WWE ring, but it seems to be a popular move with the crowd here tonight!"

"This thing is descending into chaos, Cole! All the Divas are fighting on the outside of the ring!"

"You're right, partner, but look at what is happening in the ring! Mickie James just hit the Mick Kick on Melina and has her covered for the pin!"

"One...two...three! Mickie James has won it for her team! What a match, Cole!"

"The referee raises Mickie's arm in victory as her teammates climb into the ring to join her!"

"That was one of the greatest Diva matches I have ever seen!"

"You're right, partner. But you can see just how much this match meant to these women!"

"All 10 of these Divas gave their all in this matchup, but unfortunately, only one team could come out on top."

"What are you talking about, Cole? Somebody has to lose!"

"Of course they look happy, Cole, you idiot! They just won the match!"

"Mickie James, Torrie Wilson, Kelly Kelly, Michele McCool and Maria celebrate their victory here at *Survivor Series 2007*!"

"I still can't get over that kiss from Mickie!"

"From the looks of it, JBL, neither can Melina!"

"Victoria sure doesn't look happy as she and her team mates make their way up the ramp!"

"I am sure somewhere down the line, Phoenix and James are going to cross paths, and I, for one, can't wait to see it!"

"And there you see Beth Phoenix pointing out to Mickie James that although she may have been on the losing side tonight, she is still the champ!"

Name:	The Great Khali
Height:	7'0 1/2"
Weight:	408 lbs.
From:	India
Move:	Khali Vise Grip

Name:	Hornswoggle
Height:	4'5"
Weight:	115 lbs.
From:	Oshkosh, WI
Move:	Tadpole Splash

Since being revealed as Mr. McMahon's illegitimate offspring last September on *Raw*, Hornswoggle has delighted fans with his un-McMahon-like shenanigans. His antics could be cut short at *Survivor Series*, though.

As a result of the WWE Chairman's ever-sadistic "tough love" philosophy, the littlest member of the McMahon clan must come face-to... knee with the largest athlete in sports-entertainment, the 7-foot-3, 420-pound Great Khali.

Khali has been a terror since he lost the World Heavyweight Championship to Batista at *Unforgiven*. In fact, his destructive anger seems to grow with each passing week – unfortunately for the leprechaunic McMahon, who has been trying to prove his worth to his father since finding out which family tree he fell from. The former Cruiserweight Champion will need a power far greater than the luck of the Irish if he hopes to escape *Survivor Series* with all of his limbs in their proper places.

NSWOGGLE VS. GREAT KHALI

AND THERE'S THE BELL!

"Well, Cole, here we go with one of the strangest matches I have ever seen in WWE!"

"I don't think there has ever been a match where the two participants have been so different!"

"Here comes Hornswoggle's father and brother, Mr. McMahon and Shane McMahon!"

"It was Mr. McMahon that made this match for his son. You have to wonder why McMahon would put Hornswoggle in a situation like this!"

"That is simple, Cole! Hornswoggle has to prove that he has what it takes to be called a McMahon. It's all about tough love!"

"Tough love is right, JBL. Hornswoggle is going to get killed out there tonight!"

"Historically, Hornswoggle is one of WWE's smallest performers, Cole!"

"Hornswoggle sure does look pleased to be here though, Cole!"

"Well, that's not surprising. *Survivor Series* is historically one of WWE's biggest events!"

"It looks like the McMahons are giving Hornswoggle some advice out there!"

"All the advice in the world is not going to help Hornswoggle once the Great Khali steps inside the ring!"

"Here he comes now, JBL! The former World Heavyweight Champion is on his way to the ring!"

"Look at this, Cole! Is Mr. McMahon standing up to The Great Khali?"

"Perhaps McMahon has finally realised that putting his son in a match with this beast is just plain cruel!"

"Khali is a monster under normal circumstances, but this could get ugly fast!"

"This really does not need to happen. Somebody do something!"

"The McMahons sure don't look too happy!"

"Just look at the size of this guy! He is unbelievable!"

"He makes Mr. McMahon look small, and McMahon is in no way a small guy!"

"In fact, they are making a hasty retreat to the outside of the ring!"

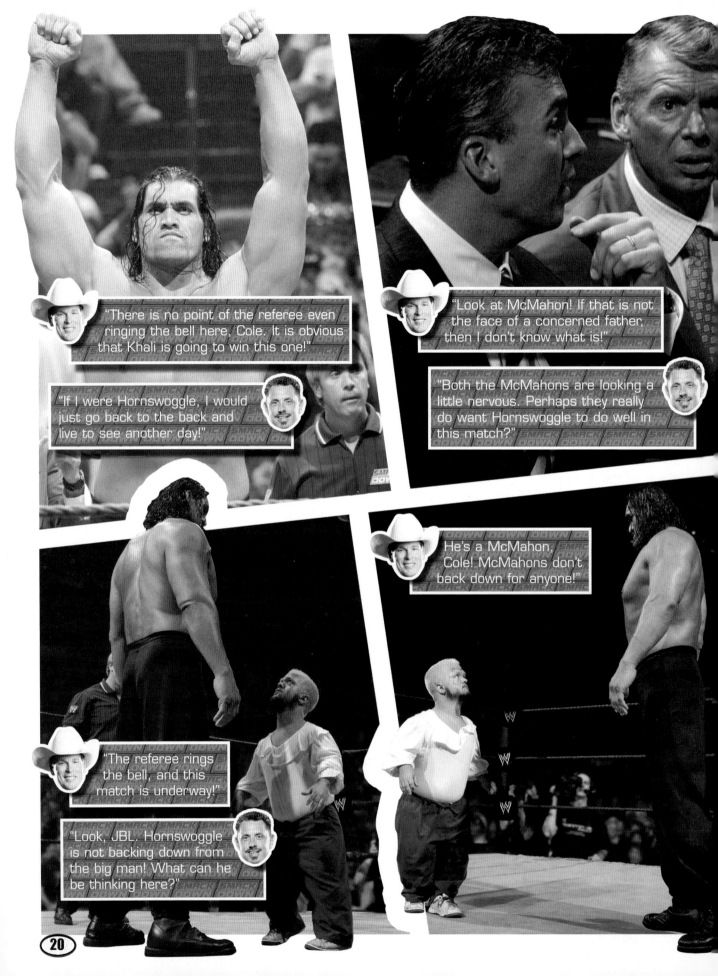

"There is no point of the referee even ringing the bell here, Cole. It is obvious that Khali is going to win this one!"

"If I were Hornswoggle, I would just go back to the back and live to see another day!"

"Look at McMahon! If that is not the face of a concerned father, then I don't know what is!"

"Both the McMahons are looking a little nervous. Perhaps they really do want Hornswoggle to do well in this match?"

He's a McMahon, Cole! McMahons don't back down for anyone!"

"The referee rings the bell, and this match is underway!"

"Look, JBL. Hornswoggle is not backing down from the big man! What can he be thinking here?"

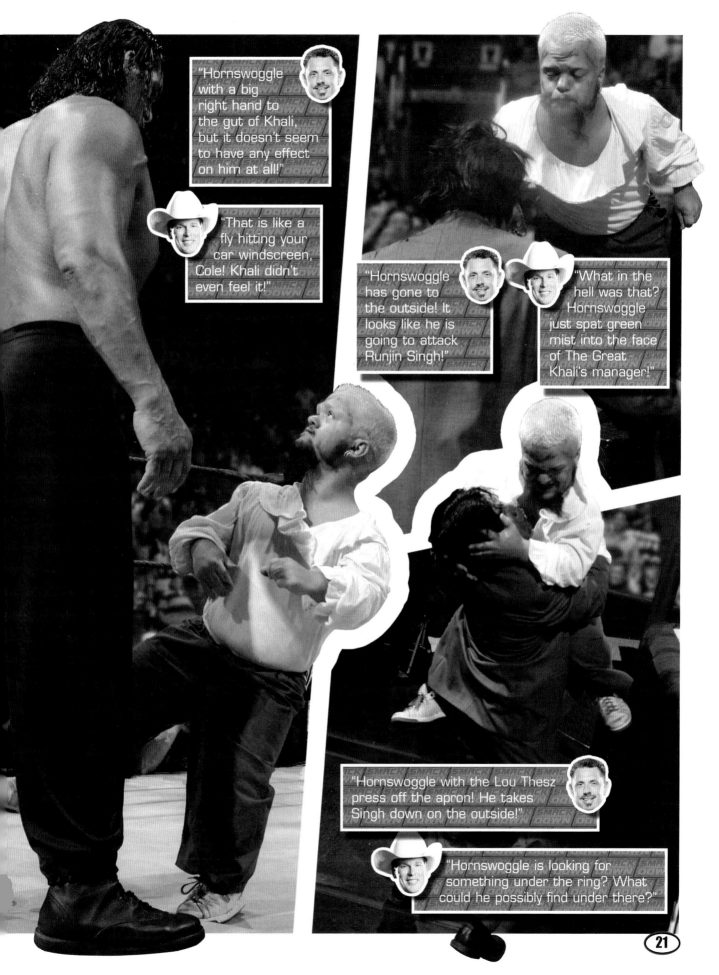

"Hornswoggle with a big right hand to the gut of Khali, but it doesn't seem to have any effect on him at all!"

"That is like a fly hitting your car windscreen, Cole! Khali didn't even feel it!"

"Hornswoggle has gone to the outside! It looks like he is going to attack Runjin Singh!"

"What in the hell was that? Hornswoggle just spat green mist into the face of The Great Khali's manager!"

"Hornswoggle with the Lou Thesz press off the apron! He takes Singh down on the outside!"

"Hornswoggle is looking for something under the ring? What could he possibly find under there?"

21

"Hornswoggle has the shillelagh! Surely he is not going to attack Khali with it!"

"I don't think Hornswoggle could swing that thing hard enough for it to have any effect on the giant!"

"Hornswoggle is a braver man than I! Check him out JBL, he is going after Khali with the Shillelagh!"

"Brave or stupid, Cole? Those shots are not doing anything to Khali!"

"You're right, JBL. Khali just swatted Hornswoggle away with one of his massive, boulder-like hands!"

"Hornswoggle goes down, and goes down hard!"

22

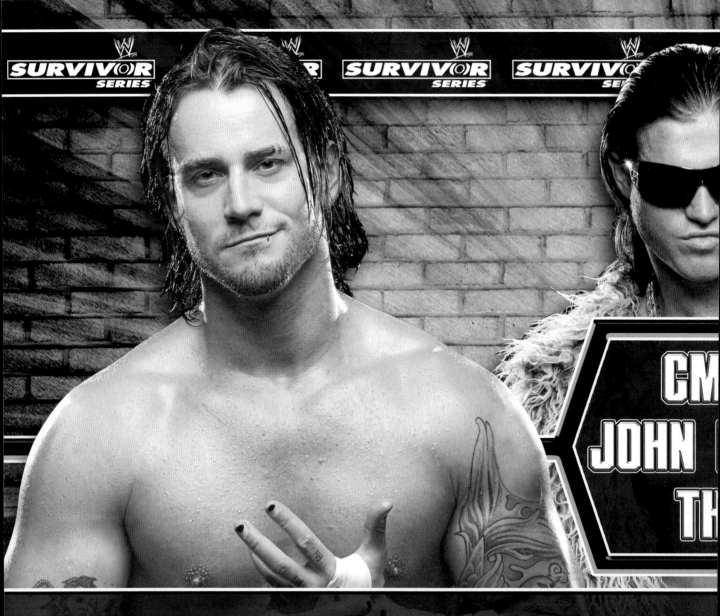

CM
JOHN
TH

After the world witnessed the hat trick that altered the fate of No. 1 contender John Morrison on ECW, General Manager Armando Estrada made an executive decision regarding the ECW Championship and *Survivor Series*. Following the conclusion of the ECW Championship Match (and the ensuing brawl), Estrada has announced that CM Punk will face both The Miz and Morrison in a Triple Threat Match, live on pay-per-view.

In the past two weeks, Punk has battled the self-proclaimed "Chick Magnet" and the "Shaman of Sexy" in singles competition with the gold at stake. Though he secured victories on both occasions, Punk's reign is at a greater risk in a match where he doesn't even need to be pinned to lose the gold.

Can the "Straight-Edge Superstar" be able to hold off the WWE Tag Team Champions and retain his ECW title?

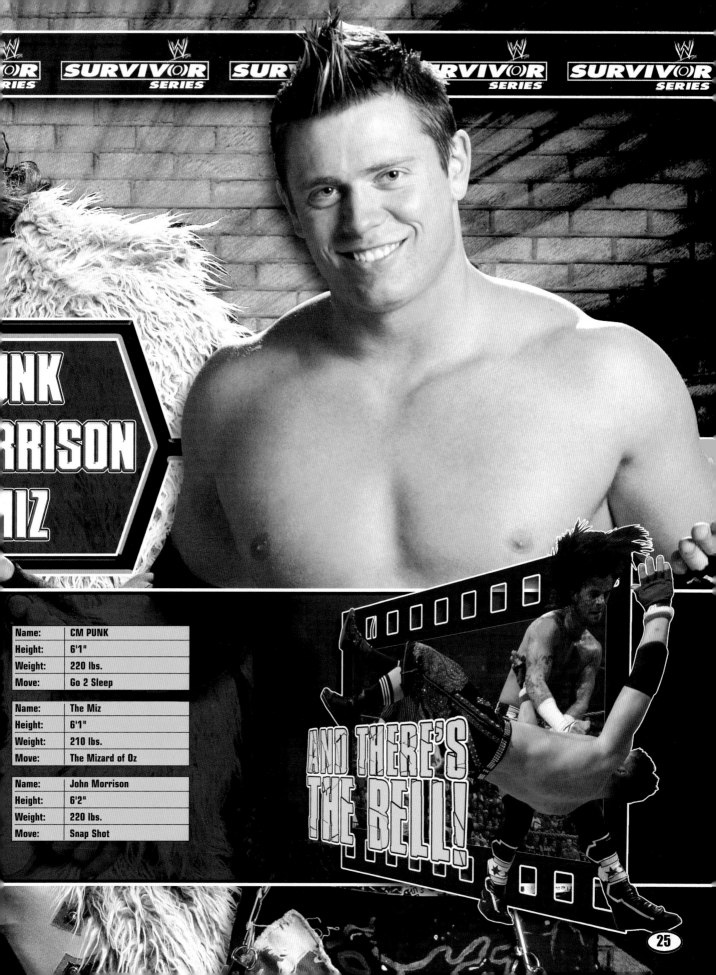

NK
RRISON
MIZ

Name:	CM PUNK
Height:	6'1"
Weight:	220 lbs.
Move:	Go 2 Sleep

Name:	The Miz
Height:	6'1"
Weight:	210 lbs.
Move:	The Mizard of Oz

Name:	John Morrison
Height:	6'2"
Weight:	220 lbs.
Move:	Snap Shot

AND THERE'S THE BELL!

"CM Punk is incredibly popular with this crowd here tonight, and it is easy to see why!"

"Well there he is, Joey! It's the ECW Champion, CM Punk!"

"For the first time ever, the ECW Championship will be defended at *Survivor Series* in a Triple Threat Match!"

"Punk is the most exciting young Superstar in WWE today, and I am proud to have him as our ECW Champion."

"He is not going to have it easy tonight though, Joey! Tonight he has to take on both John Morrison and the Miz."

"You have to think that those two guys are going to try to work together to take out the champ!"

"Morrison and Miz are current WWE Tag Team Champions and both great Superstars in their own right."

"You're right, Tazz. This could end up being a handicap match!"

"And here comes Miz! I can't stand this guy on a personal level, Joey, but he is a great up-and-coming talent."

"I have to agree with you on both those points, Tazz. I could not imagine a worse ECW Champion than Miz."

"Look at this guy, Joey! John Morrison is making his way to the ring!"

"Morrison is a former ECW Champion, and you can be sure that he wants the title back in his possession!"

"Like you said before, Joey, Miz and Morrison are the WWE Tag Team Champions, so they are both used to carrying the gold!"

"I just hope that CM Punk can overcome the odds here tonight!"

"Morrison and Miz continue to double team CM Punk here with punches to the gut of the champion!"

"Miz is working over Punk's lower back and neck with a Cobra Clutch-like manoeuvre."

"Look at Miz firing away with lefts and rights to the champ!"

"That is really going to wear the champion down! This doesn't look good, Joey!"

"Miz rolls to the outside and John Morrison hits him with a baseball slide that sends his tag team partner crashing into the barrier!"

Well, I guess that is the end of that partnership!"

"Don't count the champ out too soon, Tazz! Look at that kick from CM Punk!"

"Punk just came from out of nowhere with a boot to the face of Miz!"

"Morrison hits the backbreaker on Punk and stretches the champ's spine!"

"Morrison has Punk tied up in some sort of chokehold here!"

"The human body is not meant to bend that way, Joey!"

"Punk really needs to escape. This hold will put you to sleep in a second!"

"Punk's battling his way back up to his feet. Punk with a series of kicks to the challenger!"

"Punk is finally getting in some offence in this match!"

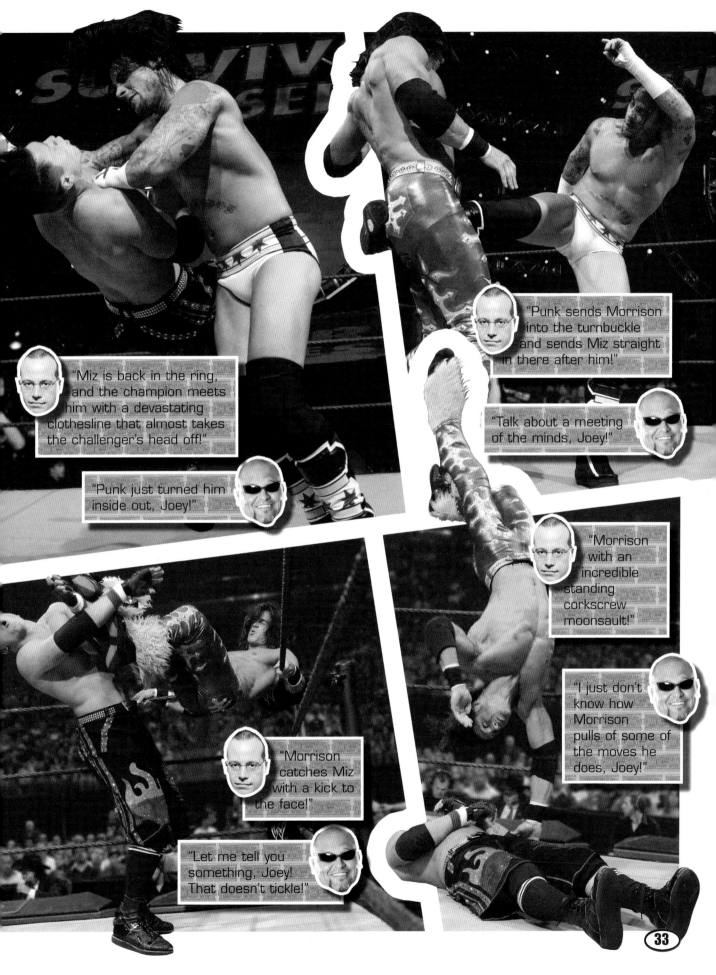

"Miz is back in the ring, and the champion meets him with a devastating clothesline that almost takes the challenger's head off!"

"Punk just turned him inside out, Joey!"

"Punk sends Morrison into the turnbuckle and sends Miz straight in there after him!"

"Talk about a meeting of the minds, Joey!"

"Morrison with an incredible standing corkscrew moonsault!"

"I just don't know how Morrison pulls of some of the moves he does, Joey!"

"Morrison catches Miz with a kick to the face!"

"Let me tell you something, Joey! That doesn't tickle!"

"Morrison is still down on the outside after that hurricanrana!"

"And he doesn't look too happy!"

"CM Punk, on the other hand, looks overjoyed to have retained the ECW Championship!"

"That is a problem for another time. Tonight, here at *Survivor Series*, CM Punk reigns supreme as ECW Champion!"

"I don't know how Miz and John Morrison are going to get over this and continue to work together as a tag team."

"What a great match, Joey! I have never seen anything like it!"

BAT
UNDE
SUR

The Anima

U ndertaker and Batista had faced each other four times leading to their match at *Survivor Series*, and both men were well aware of how dangerous the other could be. Undertaker defeated Batista at *WrestleMania 23* and Batista defeated the "Deadman" at *Cyber Sunday*. The other two confrontations resulted in draws, showing just how well the two monsters are matched.

Undertaker challenged Batista for the World Heavyweight Championship on *SmackDown* the week following his loss to the "Animal" at *Cyber Sunday*. Being the champion, Batista did not have to accept the match at *Survivor Series*, but having the respect he does for Undertaker and the challenge he represents, Batista agreed to the showdown.

Then again, perhaps Batista was a bit hasty in accepting the challenge, especially after Undertaker uttered the four words that sends shivers down any WWE Superstar's spine. Hell in a Cell has earned every bit of its standing as the most dangerous match in sports-entertainment.

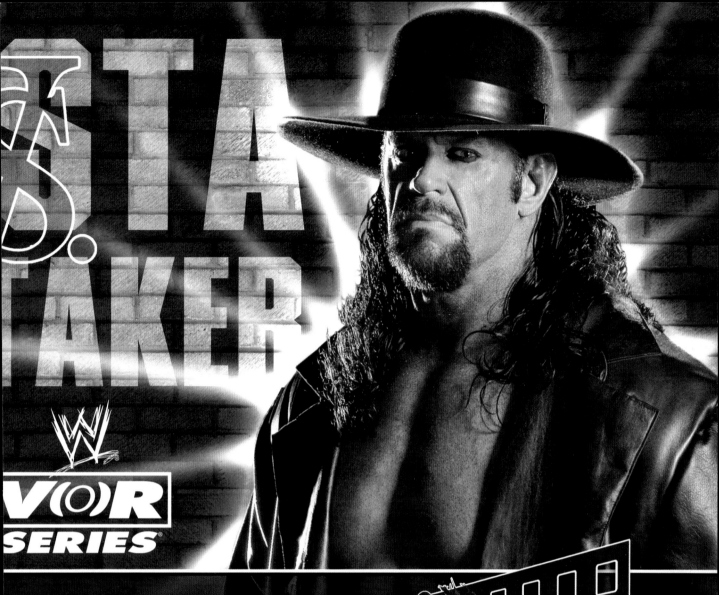

S.TA. TAKER

WWE SURVIVOR SERIES

★★★★★★★★★★★★★★★★★★★★★★★★★★★★★★★
The 20-foot-high, 30'-by-30' structure was built on a foundation of broken bones and shortened careers.

But while the fans remain divided over who to cheer for in the main event, they agree on one thing: the showdown will make history.

Name:	Batista
Height:	6'6"
Weight:	290 lbs.
Hometown:	Washington, D.C.
Move:	Batisa Bomb

Name:	Undertaker
Height:	6'10"
Weight:	295 lbs.
Hometown:	Houston, TX
Move:	Tombstone Piledriver

AND THERE'S THE BELL!

"Well, JBL, it's time for the main event of the evening. Batista against Undertaker for the World Heavyweight Championship!"

"Not only that, Cole! The title is on the line inside the most demonic structure known to man, Hell In A Cell!"

"Batista can not afford to be intimidated by Undertaker though, can he, partner?"

"I know just what you mean, JBL. It really is an impressive sight seeing the 'Deadman' make his way to the ring."

"The challenger, Undertaker, is slowly making his way to the ring, where Batista is already waiting for him."

"Undertaker is the master of mind games, and his entrance is just another part of that!"

"I think if there is one person on this planet that is not intimidated by Undertaker, it is the man standing in the ring right now, the World Heavyweight Champion, Batista."

"Every time I see Undertaker walking to the ring it gives me goose bumps, Cole!"

"Looking at the 'Animal,' I think you might be right, JBL. He certainly doesn't seem phased by the situation."

"Hell In A Cell can shorten, or even end careers. The match is just so brutal!"

"Undertaker and Batista know each other so well by now. They have fought many battles, but none have been as dangerous as the one they are about to enter into tonight!"

"And Undertaker is a veteran of this kind of match. I have to give him the advantage in this thing!"

"The match is underway and Undertaker catches the champion with a huge clothesline!"

"This is not going to be pretty, Cole!"

"Undertaker has gone for the steel chair early in this match, which is totally legal!"

"But Batista cuts him off with a spear before Undertaker can use the steel!"

"Undertaker with Batista on the outside. Undertaker just rammed Batista face first into the steel steps!"

"Both men are on the outside and Undertaker is throwing those devastating lefts and rights that he is so well known for!"

"Undertaker is one of the best pure strikers in the game, Cole!"

"Undertaker will do anything it takes to win back the World Heavyweight Championship!"

"Undertaker lays Batista on the ring apron and has him set up for that guillotine legdrop he likes so much!"

"Both men are back in the ring and Batista takes Undertaker down with another spear!"

"What impact, Cole! How anyone gets up after that move, I'll never know!"

"The momentum in this match keeps swinging back and forth!"

"Batista whips Undertaker into the ropes and catches him with a thunderous clothesline!"

"Both these Superstars are back on the outside, and here comes Undertaker with the steel steps!"

"I think Batista has been busted open, Cole!"

"But look, Cole! Batista uses the cage to pull himself up and kicks the steel steps back into the face of the 'Deadman'!"

"Just look at the champion! He has lost a lot of blood and must be exhausted!"

"Batista uses the steel steps, and now Undertaker is busted open, too!"

"This is where Batista can prove that he is a true champion and dig down deep to pull something special out of the bag."

"We said at the start of this match that it was going to be brutal, and these two Superstars are proving us right!"

41

"Undertaker and Batista slowly make their way back into the ring and... Undertaker has Batista in the Last Ride!"

"Last Ride! LAST RIDE!"

"If Undertaker hits this move, it will all be over!"

"Undertaker goes for the pin! 1...2... Batista kicks out at two!"

"Undertaker pulls Batista back up to his feet, and it looks like he is going for the chokeslam!"

"Undertaker may be looking for another Last Ride here!"

"Undertaker hits the chokeslam and goes for another pin! 1...2... Again, Batista kicks out! How is he doing this?"

"But Batista reverses it and hits Undertaker with a spinebuster! How is this match going to end?"

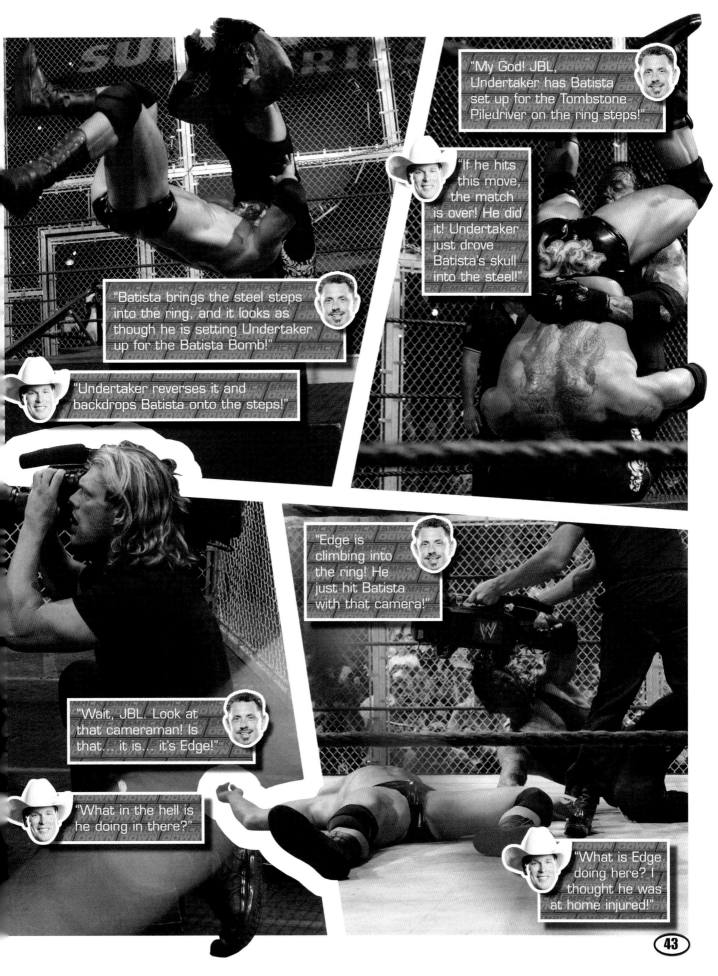

"My God! JBL, Undertaker has Batista set up for the Tombstone Piledriver on the ring steps!"

"If he hits this move, the match is over! He did it! Undertaker just drove Batista's skull into the steel!"

"Batista brings the steel steps into the ring, and it looks as though he is setting Undertaker up for the Batista Bomb!"

"Undertaker reverses it and backdrops Batista onto the steps!"

"Edge is climbing into the ring! He just hit Batista with that camera!"

"Wait, JBL. Look at that cameraman! Is that... it is... it's Edge!"

"What in the hell is he doing in there?"

"What is Edge doing here? I thought he was at home injured!"

"Batista is being helped to the back by two referees!"

"You can bet that this is not the way Batista wanted to retain his title!"

"You are right, JBL. I am pretty sure that Batista didn't have a clue what was happening. He was knocked out cold!"

"And how pleased does Edge look with himself. What a despicable act!"

"I'm sure we will see Undertaker and Batista go at it again somewhere down the line!"

"Edge is back with a vengeance, here at *Survivor Series*!"